Usborne Detective Guides
CLUES &
SUSPECTS

Anne Civardi
Illustrated by Colin King

Consultant: Donald Rumbelow
Series Editor: Heather Amery

About This Book

A good detective finds and uses all sorts of clues—a hair, a button, faint footprints or even a thread—to track down suspects. He trains himself to spot crooks, question witnesses and to judge if someone is innocent or guilty.

This book tells you how to be a good detective. It shows you how to make an identi-flick book and identi-sketches to help you find out what a suspect looks like. There are lots of words, called identi-words, to help you describe a suspect, too. The stories in the book show you how detectives go about their work to solve crimes.

This book also shows you the ways in which crooks work and the cunning tricks they use. There are lots of puzzles to do and mysteries to solve.

First published in 1979 by Usborne Publishing Ltd. 20 Garrick Street, London WC2 9BJ, England

No part of this publication may be reproduced, stored in a retrieval system or transmitted in any form or by any means, electronic,

Printed in Belgium

The name Usborne and the device are Trade Marks of Usborne Publishing Ltd.

© Usborne Publishing Ltd 1979

mechanical, photocopying, recording or otherwise, without the prior permission of the publisher.

CLUES & SUSPECTS

Contents

Detective Work

Good detectives are quick-witted, sharp-eyed and always on the look-out for anything suspicious. They must learn to do all sorts of things, such as looking for clues, questioning people and tracking down suspects. Here are some ways to be a good detective.

Look in all good hiding places when you are searching for clues.

Remember—the most unlikely things may turn out to be important clues.

Even the craftiest crook may leave a clue at the scene of a crime. Check everything you find very carefully. It may lead you to the villain.

Be on the look-out for suspicious characters and train yourself to remember their faces. You never know where you may see them again.

Wear clothes that blend with your surroundings when you are tracking a crook. Tiptoe very quietly to get as close to him as you can.

Question the people who saw a crook in action. They are called witnesses.

If you see someone who is acting suspiciously, ask him what he is doing.

Setting Up an Office

Before you can do any detective business, you need an office to work from. Here you can store your detective gear and set up crafty traps for crooks. Some may help you to guess if a suspect is innocent or guilty. Look at Detective Dodd's office to get some tips.

POSITION MIRROR TO SHOW VIEW AT WINDOW

BELL

FINGERPRINT FILE

MO'S

IDENT KIT

HANG TAPE TO MEASURE SUSPECT'S HEIGHT

SPRINKLE TALCUM POWDER NEAR DOOR TO TRAP FOOTPRINTS

CRIME RECO

USE OLD CHEST OF DRAWERS AS FILING CABINET

FACE CLOCK TOWARDS YOU

KEEP DISGUISES OUT OF SIGHT

SECRET HEIGHT MEASURES

KEEP TAPE RECORDER AND MICROPHONE HIDDEN FROM VIEW

Sit with your back to the window. Then, when you question a suspect, you can see his face clearly. Hang something above the door which makes a noise when the door is opened, even a crack. Make sure you can see what is going on behind you—a crook may be spying on you.

NEIGHBOURHOOD MAP

TED

WANTED

SIT WITH BACK TOWARDS WINDOW

REPORTS

RECENT CRIMES

TELEPHONE BOOK

SECRET FOOT ALARM BUTTON

Give-Aways

Even if he is in disguise, a crook may give himself away by a habit, such as pulling his ears or scratching his kneecaps. Here are all sorts of different habits that people have. They may help you to recognize a crook.

Whistling

Drumming Fingers

Biting Fingernails

Cracking Knuckles

Scratching Kneecaps

Tapping Feet

Wrapped Legs

Biting Glasses

Stroking Beard

Twirling Moustache

Twitch and Tugging Eyebrows

Cigar Smoking

Chewing Gum

Picking Teeth **Grinding Teeth** **Pulling Earlobe**

Spot the Clues

A cunning thief has burgled this room. The picture below shows what the room looked like before the burglary. The one on the right is the same room afterwards. How many clues can

you spot which tell you a thief has broken in?
What has he stolen? Has he replaced anything
with a fake? How many things has he disturbed?
You should be able to find at least 20 clues.

Hijack

Detectives have been tipped off that four dangerous crooks are planning to hijack a boat to escape the country. Quickly they set up a clever trap to catch them.

Wearing disguises, the detectives take up their positions. They have been after this gang for many months. Now is their big chance to catch them. Can you work out how they do it?

DISGUISED RADIO TRANSMITTER

DETECTIVE READY TO SIGNAL POLICE LAUNCH

CROOK DISGUISED AS CREWMAN

DETECTIVE FROGMAN

POLICE HELICOPTER

POLICE LAUNCH READY FOR ACTION

DETECTIVE FROGMEN

DETECTIVES DISGUISED AS FISHERMEN

DETECTIVE DISGUISED AS TOURIST

What Happens

While the fishermen block the path of the boat, a frogman wraps rope round its propellers to stop them working. Then the diver signals the police launch to swoop. The fisherman on the quay, using a radio disguised as a fishing rod, radios the helicopter to fly in closer and lower men on to the deck. The crooks are arrested.

How Crooks Work

Some crooks stick to the same sort of crime and do it the same way each time. This is called their modus operandi (M.O.) or way of working. A good detective keeps a special M.O.

Bones

Bones gives the guard dog a big, juicy bone when he burgles a house. This keeps it quiet and happy.

Brusher

Brusher is a very tidy crook. He always washes away his foot and finger prints after a crime.

Fred the Feet

Before each job, Fred the Feet takes off his socks and shoes. But his bare footprints give him away.

Stuffer

This crook is nicknamed Stuffer because he eats so much. He drops bits of food wherever he goes.

file in his office. Sometimes he gives each crook a nickname to help him remember how he works and to catch him quickly. Here are the M.O.'s of some crooks who burgle houses.

Gumboy

Every time he blows open a safe, Gumboy uses bits of pink bubblegum to stick the fuse to the door.

Pyramid Pete

Pyramid Pete always lays a trap in the house that he burgles. This is to trip up the owner.

Junior

Junior takes his mother with him to keep watch. But she leaves bits of embroidery behind.

The Count

The Count only steals from very rich people. He pretends to be the owner of each house he burgles.

15

Break-In

Late one night, a jewellery shop is burgled. At the scene of the crime, Detective Trapper searches for clues left behind by the robber. Careful not to disturb anything, he circles the room and makes a note of what he sees.

Searching for Clues

Don't touch anything with your fingertips until the room has been dusted for fingerprints.

Look for prints on windows and drawers. But use a stick or ruler to open and close them.

Although the villain has got away with a sackful of diamond rings and bracelets, he has been clumsy. How many clues can you spot which may give him away? Turn over to see what evidence Détective Trapper finds.

Search everywhere. Even tiny clues—a hair or a matchstick—may help to identify a crook.

Always have a notebook handy. Talk to the witnesses and write down everything they tell you.

now turn over

Gathering Evidence

As soon as the shop is dusted for prints, Detectives Trapper and Dodd get down to work. They collect clues which will help them to catch the crook. Each piece of evidence is put in a plastic bag and carefully labelled. Later it will go to the lab for examination.

The hairs on this greasy comb may show what colour hair the crook has, or if it is dyed.

A broken electric drill is found beside the safe. But the serial number has been filed off.

Dodd takes a photograph of a dusty footprint. He notices that there are strange marks across it.

Trapper collects the dust from the footprint for examination. It may show where the crook has been.

The crook left a message. Trapper measures it to get an idea of how tall the crook is.

As the crook climbed through the window, a few threads from his jacket caught on a nail.

Dodd uses a special brush and powder to show up a set of fingerprints. Now they will be photographed.

The M.O. file may record crooks who work like this. They cut holes in windows to reach the latch.

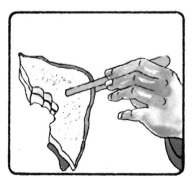

The crook may be traced through the teethmarks on the ham sandwich that he left behind.

Dodd examines the plastic sandwich wrapper for fingerprints. He should pick it up with tweezers.

At the Lab

EXAMINING DRILL UNDER INFRA-RED LAMP

BRUCE BUNGLE (THE SUSPECT)

TESTING SOIL FROM SUSPECT'S SHOES

B. BUNGLE M.O.S

SUSPECT'S M.O. FILE

EXAMINING THREADS

At the lab, the evidence from the jewellery shop robbery is examined. It looks as if the well-known, but clumsy crook, Bruce Bungle has been stealing again. Bruce, who has been brought in for questioning, has his photo taken for the criminal record files.

Bruce must be the burglar because . . .
1. Soil from his shoes matches the soil found on the shop carpet.
2. The cuts in his shoe soles match the ones in the footprint photos.
3. A plaster cast of the sandwich show that the teethmarks are Bruce's.

4. Bruce's bleached hair is exactly the same as the hairs found on the comb.
5. The threads match the material of his jacket.
6. His M.O. file states that he always leaves messages after a crime, and cuts glass out of a window to break in.

7. The serial number on the drill shows up in a special light. The shop which sold it to Bruce can now be traced.
8. The fingerprints on the glass are Bruce's.
9. A puzzle is solved—the fingerprints on the sandwich wrapper belong to Detective Dodd.

Is This the Crook?

Crooks often try to change their looks. But their faces, feet and clothes sometimes give them away. A good detective looks carefully for things that will tell him about a person. What can you learn about the man below?

His hair is dyed—the roots are black. He has shaved off his beard—the skin underneath is paler than the rest of his face. His rumpled clothes may mean he is sleeping out of doors. Perhaps he is on the run from prison.

He wears his watch on his right hand—he may be left-handed. His broken nose and battered ears may mean he is a boxer. His suit and shoes are too small—maybe he has stolen them. The tattoo on his hand may show that he is a sailor.

Things to look out for

This man usually wears glasses—look at the mark on his nose. His even, white teeth must be false.

This man often wears a hat—maybe he wears a uniform at work. The scar on his cheek is new.

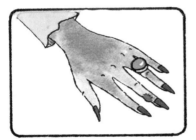

This woman is married and writes with her left hand. She takes care of herself and may be rich.

This man works with his hands. He smokes a lot and bites his nails—he must be a nervous person.

This man must ride a bike. The pencils in his pocket may mean that he does a lot of paper work.

Feet often give people away. Tall people usually have big feet. Short people have small ones.

Training Dogs

Dogs often help detectives in their work. Petal is being trained to track down and catch crooks. She was chosen for detective work because she is a brave and clever dog. Before she can go out on patrol, Petal must learn to do whatever her handler tells her—on and off a lead, before and after a chase. It will take many months of hard training.

First of all, Petal learns to walk to 'heel' beside her handler's left knee, like this.

Then she learns to obey orders, such as 'stand', 'sit' and 'lie down'.

If her handler tells her to 'stay', Petal must not move until she is told to 'come'.

An important lesson Petal learns is to fetch things for her handler. This is called 'retrieving'.

If she hears the order to 'speak', Petal must bark. She should stop when her handler says 'quiet'.

Petal is trained to climb up things which are too high to jump. This is one of the hardest exercises.

In case she has to chase a crook, Petal must know how to jump over low things like walls and logs.

Petal must be very fit and move quickly. She is taught to leap across things at least 3 m wide.

Petal is a very good swimmer. She learns how to fetch things that are floating in the water.

She must not be afraid of loud noises. One day she may have to chase a crook who has a gun.

Nosework

Petal uses her nose to sniff out suspects—this is called nose-work. She can smell and hear much better than a person can.

1. PETAL SNIFFS GLOVE DROPPED BY CROOK TO GET USED TO HIS SCENT

2. PICKS UP TRAIL AND JUMPS HEDGE HERE

3. LOSES SCENT CROSSING PATH BECAUSE OF RECENT PASSER-BY. HER SCENT STRONGER THAN CROOK'S

4. PICKS UP CROOK'S SCENT AGAIN ON PIECE OF HIS SHIRT

5. CROSSES FIELD. IS NOT DISTRACTED BY SHEEP AND NOISY TRACTOR

Catching the Suspect

If the suspect stands still, Petal circles round him, growling.

If he tries to escape, she grips his arm and holds on with her teeth.

A crook is on the run. This picture shows how Petal picks up his scent. Follow the trail to find out where the crook is hiding.

8 LOSES TRAIL OVER BUSY ROAD. A PASSING CAR HAS SPOILED THE SCENT

9 PICKS UP STRONG SCENT. CROOK MUST BE CLOSE

10 FINDS CROOK IN DERELICT BUILDING. CLIMBS WALL TO TRAP HIM

7 PICKS UP EARTH SCENT WHERE CROOK HAS TRODDEN ON GRASS. SOIL NOW CARRIED ON THE CROOK'S SHOES

6 PETAL LOSES SCENT CROSSING STREAM. CROOK MUST HAVE WADED ACROSS

Petal barks to let her handler know where she has cornered the crook.

The handler arrives and arrests the suspect. Now Petal can sit and rest.

Framed (The Case of the False Evidence)

Krusties, the well-known art dealers, are holding their yearly auction in two days' time. A very valuable painting is to be sold.

Larry Loyal, Audrey Applecart and Harold Hoe who work for Krusties, are the only three who know about the painting. They have arrived to collect it from its owner, Sir Timothy Trumble.

Inside Sir Timothy's stately home, Larry Loyal slips a cheap painting over the real one to disguise it. He is watched by Harold Hoe, Audrey Applecart and Sir Timothy Trumble.

Larry takes the painting home to guard until the auction. He hangs it above his fireplace.

But, during the night, the painting is stolen. Detective Trapper arrives to investigate the crime.

Back in his office, he looks at the clues found at the scene of the crime. 'Only four people knew where the painting was that night', he thinks. 'One of them must be the thief. But who is it?'.

The Four Suspects

Timothy Trumble

Has he stolen the painting to get the $1,000,000 it is insured for? And kept the painting for himself?

Larry Loyal

Larry works hard, but he does not earn much money. Perhaps he is fed up with being so poor?

Audrey Applecart

Miss Audrey Applecart lives alone with her dog. Nobody knows very much about her.

Harold Hoe

Harold has been at Krusties for ten years. He has a stiff leg because of a motor accident.

now turn over 29

Framed (2)

After questioning the four suspects, Trapper is sure that Sir Timothy is not the thief. He flew to Africa before the painting disappeared. And Larry must be innocent. His feet are much bigger than the prints that have been found. All the evidence points to Harold Hoe . . .

'Your hat, footprints and pipe were found at Larry's house', says Trapper to Harold Hoe. 'You must have stolen the painting'.

'But I was not there', pleads Harold. 'Wait, I remember. I lost some things when my house was burgled last month'.

Is Harold telling the truth? Trapper looks in his crime complaints book to see if the burglary has been reported.

TUESDAY SEPT 4
4.30 AM
BURGLARY AT
10 IVY ROAD
OWNER:
HAROLD HOE

ARTICLES STOLEN
GOLD WATCH
SILVER FRAME
CANTEEN OF
SILVER
PIPE, COMB, SHOES
GARDEN HAT

Sure enough, it has. Among the stolen things were a hat, a pipe and a pair of old shoes. Has Harold Hoe been framed?

Puzzled, Trapper goes back to Larry's house. 'Harold is too fat to get through that window', he thinks. 'He could not climb this wall with his stiff leg. And where are his walking stick marks? These are dog prints. Ah! Miss Applecart has a dog'.

As he expected, Trapper finds the painting at Audrey's house. 'Yes', she confesses, 'I burgled Harold's house. Then I

wore his shoes and left his hat and pipe when I stole the painting. I hoped you would think Harold was the thief'.

Which is the Getaway Car?

One evening, a crook smuggled a case full of gold watches through customs at a big airport. Five people saw him drive off in a green car.

A customs officer said that the car had a dent on the right wing. The steering wheel was on the left. An L, S and a 2 were somewhere on the numberplate. The left headlight was broken.

An old lady thought that a Y, K and a 4 were on the numberplate. The car had two doors.

A boy scout said that a front hub cap was missing. The car had four doors.

A businessman stated that the dent was on the left wing. The right headlight was broken.

A porter thought the car had two side mirrors, one windscreen wiper and an aerial on the roof.

The customs officer, the boy scout and the porter were right. The old lady and businessman were wrong. Which of these is the getaway car?

Answer

Car number 3 is the getaway car.

33

Detective Disguises

Crooks often meet to talk about crimes or to hand over stolen goods. You may have to disguise yourself to get close enough to listen to their plans. Remember to wear clothes that go with your surroundings so that the crooks do not notice you or get suspicious. A hat, dark glasses or a false moustache are all very useful disguises.

1 Gardener

If the crooks meet in a park, pretend you are a gardener. As you weed, crawl as close as you can to their meeting spot.

To get very close, use a pointed stick to pick up leaves and paper. Drop paper behind you if you want to go back again.

1 Window Cleaner

To disguise yourself as a window cleaner, you need a bucket of water and a cloth. Remember to wear overalls or old clothes.

Move from one window to the next while you watch the crooks. Don't stare for too long or they might get suspicious.

1 Tourist

Disguise yourself as a tourist if the crooks meet in a hotel or club. Hold a camera and a map.

2

Pace up and down the lobby to get closer. Look at your watch as if you are waiting for someone.

1 Jogger

Pretend to be jogging if you want to follow a crook. But don't follow too closely behind him.

2

If he suddenly stops and turns round, start doing leg and arm exercises or jog on the spot.

Lurker

If the crooks meet in a crowded place, pretend you are watching traffic or resting for a while.

Street Cleaner

Clean the street while you are keeping watch on a building or house. But don't linger for too long.

On the Look-Out

Lord and Lady Tutton have invited all their rich friends to a summer ball. While everyone is dancing, a gang of crooks disguised as guests and waiters steal everything they can. Can you spot the eleven crooks and see how they are hiding the stolen things?

Door-to-Door Villains

Detectives are always on the look-out for crooks who pretend to be drain inspectors or meter readers (1). And crooks who collect for fake charities (2), or sell stolen goods (3).

Suspicious Cars

Watch out for things such as: 1. An old car with new screws on the number plate—it may be stolen. 2. A removal van without a name on the side. 3. A car full of men waiting near or outside a bank.

Identi-Flick Book

Make this flick book and use it when you
question a witness. Ask the witnesses to flick
over the strips until they find a face that looks
most like the suspect's. The face changes a
little each time you turn a strip over.

On the next four pages there are lots of
different-shaped noses, eyes, mouths and chins
to draw in the flick book.

To make the book, pin or
staple about 12 big
pieces of paper together,
like this.

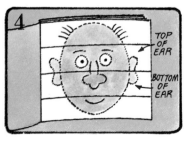

Leave the two outside
pages as covers. Cut the
ten inside pages into four
equal strips, like this.

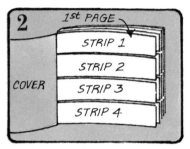

Strip 1 is for the hair,
2 for the eyebrows, eyes
and top of the nose. Strip
3 is for the nose, and 4
for the mouth and chin.

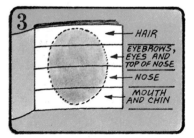

Draw a face on the four
strips of the first page
with each part of the
face on the right strip.
Draw in the ears.

5

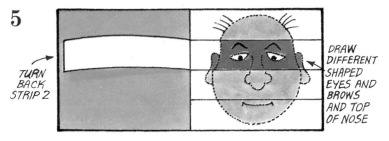

TURN BACK STRIP 2

DRAW DIFFERENT SHAPED EYES AND BROWS AND TOP OF NOSE

Turn back strip 2 and draw different shaped eyes on the next page. Match up the top of a new nose with the bottom of the nose on page one. Match up the ears and the outline of the face.

6

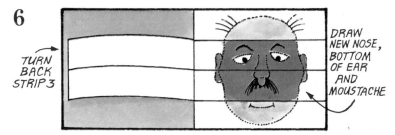

TURN BACK STRIP 3

DRAW NEW NOSE, BOTTOM OF EAR AND MOUSTACHE

Turn back strip 3 of page one and draw a different shaped nose on the next page. Try drawing in a moustache as well. Match up the ears and draw in the outline of the face.

7

TURN BACK STRIPS 1 AND 4

DRAW NEW HAIR STYLE

DRAW NEW MOUTH

To finish off the second face, turn back strips 1 and 4 and draw a new hairstyle, mouth and chin. Keep turning back the strips in this order until you have drawn a face on every page.

Know Your Crook

Watch out for crooks who have disguised themselves. Just by growing a moustache or beard, by dyeing their hair or changing their hairstyle they may look quite different. Look how this man and woman change.

Identi-Words

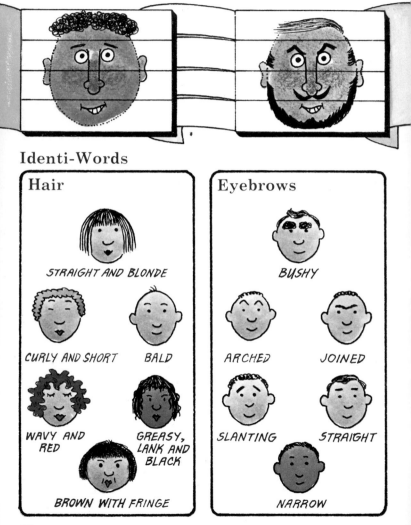

Hair

STRAIGHT AND BLONDE

CURLY AND SHORT

BALD

WAVY AND RED

GREASY, LANK AND BLACK

BROWN WITH FRINGE

Eyebrows

BUSHY

ARCHED

JOINED

SLANTING

STRAIGHT

NARROW

The identi-words below will help you describe
a person quickly and properly. Write them down
in your notebook and learn them off by heart
if you can. Try making up some identi-words
of your own too.

Moustaches

DROOPY

HANDLEBAR   BUSHY OR THICK

TOOTHBRUSH   THIN

WALRUS

Beards

POINTED

LONG   STUBBLY

BUSHY
AND
CURLY   SHORT

STRAGGLY

Identi-Words

When you spot a suspect ask yourself these
questions to help you remember exactly what he
looks like. What shape is his face and chin?
What colour and size are his eyes? What kind
of mouth and nose does he have? How long is
his hair and what colour is it?

Don't stare at him for too long. Look quickly
two or three times and jot down the answers
as soon as you get the chance. Use these
identi-words when you write your notes.

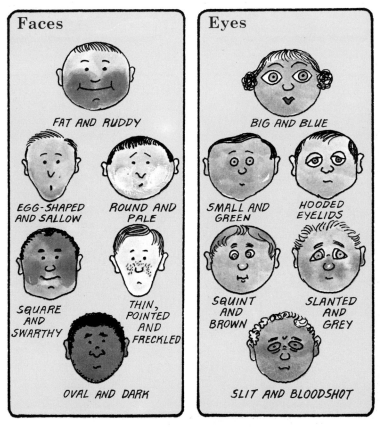

Faces

FAT AND RUDDY

EGG-SHAPED
AND SALLOW

ROUND AND
PALE

SQUARE
AND
SWARTHY

THIN,
POINTED
AND
FRECKLED

OVAL AND DARK

Eyes

BIG AND BLUE

SMALL AND
GREEN

HOODED
EYELIDS

SQUINT
AND
BROWN

SLANTED
AND
GREY

SLIT AND BLOODSHOT

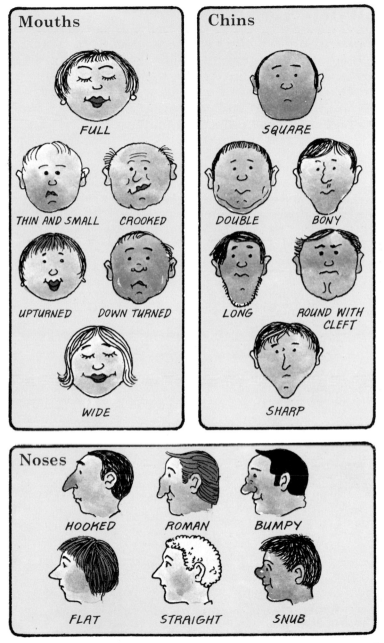

Mouths

FULL

THIN AND SMALL | CROOKED

UPTURNED | DOWN TURNED

WIDE

Chins

SQUARE

DOUBLE | BONY

LONG | ROUND WITH CLEFT

SHARP

Noses

HOOKED | ROMAN | BUMPY

FLAT | STRAIGHT | SNUB

43

Identi-Sketches

Look carefully at the shape and size of a suspect.
If you have time, make a quick sketch of him
and describe each part of his body with identi-
words. Note whether he is big or small, fat or
thin, tall or short, and what clothes he is
wearing. But remember—he may try to
disguise himself by wearing different clothes.

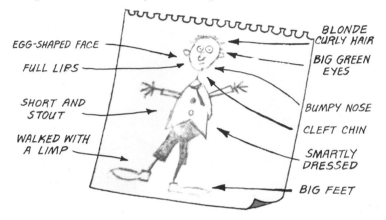

EGG-SHAPED FACE

FULL LIPS

SHORT AND
STOUT

WALKED WITH
A LIMP

BLONDE
CURLY HAIR

BIG GREEN
EYES

BUMPY NOSE

CLEFT CHIN

SMARTLY
DRESSED

BIG FEET

Look for unusual things, such as a limp, scar or very big feet. These may help you to recognize a suspect or know him when you see him again.

Remembering a Suspect

AH YES...
HE WAS
SMALL,
THIN AND
WIRY LOOKING.

HIS FACE...I REMEMBER NOW.
IT WAS THIN AND BONY WITH
A SHARP CHIN. THERE WAS
SOMETHING STRANGE ABOUT
HIS EYES. DID HE SQUINT?

44

Shapes and Sizes

FAT   THIN AND TALL   STOUT   STOOPED   SMALL

Clothes

SMART   CASUAL   FLASHY   SHABBY   SPORTY

Night Alert

Even at night, a good detective is prepared for action. He must be ready to investigate crimes and track down suspects. There are lots of crooks who only work when it is dark.

One night, when Detectives Trapper and Dodd are on duty, the telephone rings . . .

Three suspicious characters were spotted going into the Clikon Camera warehouse, Trapper is told.

Quickly, he and Dodd put on brown coats. They wear soft-soled shoes so that they can creep about quietly in the dark.

They collect the things they may need—torches, two-way radios, handcuffs and infra-red binoculars to see in the dark.

Petal, the dog, is coming too, just in case she can help. She may have to sniff out the crooks and chase them.

Silently, Trapper pulls up outside the warehouse with the car lights off. He signals to the others to keep very quiet.

He blocks off the alley with the car to stop the crooks from getting away. Then he tells everyone to take up their positions.

Dodd uses his binoculars to keep watch. Trapper creeps round the building to look for escape routes and getaway cars.

Petal and her handler stay behind to guard the fire escape. The crooks may try to use it as a quick getaway route.

Round a corner, Trapper finds a car. Does it belong to the crooks? Has it been stolen? He radios the number to HQ.

At HQ, the police use computers to trace the car. Sure enough, it was stolen a week ago. They let Trapper know at once.

now turn over

Night Alert (2)

Trapper and Dodd then creep into the warehouse. They start to hunt for the crooks.

On the ground floor, they jam open the lift. They may catch a crook escaping down the stairs.

Trapper, the expert, will search upstairs. Dodd, who is a bit scared, tiptoes down to the cellar.

On the way, he hears a noise. 'It must be the crooks', he thinks. But it is only a gurgling pipe.

CLIKON CAMERAS

Down in the cellar, he thinks he has found them. He decides to stand guard until Trapper arrives.

On the roof, Trapper sees that the fire escape is the only way down. He hears voices in the room below.

He rushes downstairs and
surprises the three crooks
at work. But they push
him over and escape.

One crook heads for the
roof and climbs down the
fire escape. But Petal
is waiting for him . . .

Another heads for the
lift but it is out of
action. Trapper catches
him without any trouble.

Now Trapper needs help—
the third crook has
disappeared. He uses his
radio to talk to Dodd.

Together they search all
over the warehouse. Has
this crafty villain got
away or is he hiding? •

They find him in the last
place they look. He is
hiding in the cold water
tank under the roof.

Who Stole the Cadillac?

One day, Gloria Burger, wife of the American Ambassador, her mother Amy Potts, and her son Hiram Burger Jnr. see a crook driving off in the family car, a big Cadillac. All three see him clearly and give his description to Detective Dodd. They say he is short and thin, with dark, curly hair, a black beard and big,

The Line-Up

AMY POTTS

POLICE OFFICER

A WITNESS ONLY HAS ONE GO AT IDENTIFYING THE VILLAIN

THE MEN IN THE LINE-UP LOOK LIKE PERCY. THEY WERE ALL ASKED TO TAKE PART BY THE POLICE

GLORIA BURGER

EACH WITNESS SITS IN A SEPARATE ROOM UNTIL IT IS HER TURN TO IDENTIFY THE CROOK

THE SUSPECT'S LAWYER IS THERE. HE OBJECTS TO ANYTHING THAT HE THINKS IS UNFAIR

bushy eyebrows. The police, who think that the villain is Percy Pike, quickly organize an identification parade, called a line-up. The Burgers and Amy Potts come to identify the crook. But Percy, who is a cunning man, tries to fool them by changing his looks. Which of the men in the line-up is Percy Pike?

AFTER EACH WITNESS, THE SUSPECT CAN CHANGE PLACES IN THE LINE-UP

HIRAM HAS ALREADY IDENTIFIED THE CROOK. HE SITS IN ANOTHER ROOM

DETECTIVE DODD STAYS IN THE ROOM HE MUST NOT TALK OR INTERRUPT

A POLICE INSPECTOR IS IN CHARGE OF THE LINE-UP

Answer

Percy Pike is crook number 2. To change his looks, he has cut off his hair, shaved off his eyebrows and beard, hunched up his shoulders and put on high-heeled boots. To make himself look fat, he has put on lots of layers of clothes and secretly filled his cheeks with cottonwool.

Questioning Witnesses

As a detective, one of your most important jobs is to question suspects and witnesses. A witness is someone who sees a crook in action and can tell you what happened at the scene of a crime.

Questions to Ask

Different Witnesses

There are all sorts of witnesses. Some are shy—treat them gently and try to help them. Others get very excited and talk too much. Calm them down so that they tell you only the most important details.

Some, who did not see the crime at all, just want to join in the action. You must learn to spot story-tellers from real witnesses. Remember—if a witness is colour-blind, he may be wrong about the colours he saw.

It is best to question a witness in a quiet place where you will not be disturbed.

Don't hurry her when you ask her questions. Get her to tell you what happened, how close she was, how many crooks she saw and what time it was.

Try to find out what the crook looked like. Did she spot anything unusual about him, such as a limp or a scar? If she saw him clearly enough, ask her to make a quick sketch of him for you.

Remember—each witness may tell a different story. You will have to judge who is likely to get it right.

Testing Witnesses

Ask the witness to guess how far away something is. This is to find out if she can judge distances.

Ask her to guess how tall you are. If she is right, she will be right about the crook's height.

Looking for Suspects

When you have questioned each witness, you will have to check their stories and look for the suspects. You need a lot of energy and patience—it is hard work and may take time.

Check all the criminal files in your office. Search for a photograph of a crook who fits the description that the witnesses have given you.

If you have found a good set of fingerprints, see if they match any in your fingerprint file.

Remember to check your M.O. file, too—you may find a record of a crook who works the same way.

Show any identi-sketches of the suspect to people who live or work close to the crime. They may know him or have seen him lurking about.

You may find more than one person who fits the suspect's description. Before you question them, find out as much as you can about them. Always remember—many suspects are innocent.

Talk to the suspect's friends—they probably know him best.

You may pick up a few clues about his habits from his work mates.

How does he spend his spare time? Does he go to church or a club?

Find out if he has a criminal record. He may have struck before.

Questioning Suspects

There are lots of things a detective should know about questioning a suspect. It is very important not to get cross, to talk quietly and be as patient as possible. Watch out for signs, like the ones below, which might help you guess whether the suspect is innocent or guilty. Ask him to tell his story over and over again—he may slip up and change it.

Signs of Guilt

Some guilty suspects look away while you question them, or blush, get hot and angry or grow pale. But remember—not all crooks show sign of guilt.

Signs of Innocence

An innocent person may talk too much and not listen to your questions.

He may get flustered, look worried and unhappy and very uncomfortable.

Most suspects will tell you that they were somewhere else at the time of the crime. This is called an alibi. It is your job to find out if they are telling the truth. It may be very hard to break the alibi of a crook who is used to being questioned. Here is what a suspect might say.

Checking Alibis

Check the suspect's alibi as soon as you can.
If he is lying, you will probably spot a mistake
in his story. Talk to anyone who may have
seen him, but give them a few hints to help
them remember.

One suspect said he was
watching a film. Make
sure he has given you
the whole story.

Show his photo to anyone
who may have seen him,
such as the cinema
manager or ticket seller.

Another suspect said he
was in the park. Find
out what tunes the band
played while he was there.

If, as he says, he has
lunch there most days,
someone must have seen
him. Ask anyone you see.

If you are sure a suspect is guilty, go to his house. Tell him you have come to look for the loot.

Don't worry if the crook looks sure of himself. He probably thinks you will not find anything.

Search everywhere—an experienced crook finds very good hiding places for the things he steals.

If you find evidence that proves he is guilty, arrest him. Then take him back to your office.

Warn him that anything he says may be used as evidence. Then write down his confession.

Write to the end of each line so no words can be added. Get him to read and sign each page.

Tracking Crooks

A good detective uses his eyes and ears to track down crooks. He trains himself to walk quietly and keep out of sight. And he looks at everything very carefully. Tiny clues, such as a leaf, a broken twig or a matchstick, as well as footprints or trampled grass might tell him where a crook is hiding.

Listen

Stand still and listen for things, such as a snapping twig or startled bird. They might show you where a crook is hiding.

Look

Look all around you—a quick, sudden movement might give the crook away. Remember to keep yourself hidden as well.

Getting Used to the Dark

Close your eyes for about ten seconds when you go from a light place to a dark one. Then you will be able to see more quickly in the dark.

Judging Numbers

You may have to guess how many people are at the scene of a crime. If it is a big crowd, divide it into squares with your eyes. Then count the number of people in one square and multiply it by the number of squares.

Watching for Shadows

On a sunny day, a crook who is hiding behind a tree may forget about his shadow. He thinks that if he cannot see you, you cannot see him. Stand on the sunny side of the tree so that the crook does not see your shadow.

Hints for Detectives

Here is some important information that will
help you check a witness's story. Could he have
seen the detail he thinks he saw? Is he good
at guessing how far away or close things are?

How Far Away?

50 METRES
YOU CAN SEE A PERSON'S EYES AND MOUTH

100 METRES
EYES LOOK LIKE DOTS

200 METRES
YOU CAN SEE DETAILS OF DRESS, BUTTONS AND BADGES

300 METRES
A FACE LOOKS BLURRED

400 METRES
YOU CAN MAKE OUT LEG MOVEMENTS

500 METRES
YOU CAN SEE HEAD, HAT AND COLOURS OF CLOTHES

600 METRES
HEAD LOOKS LIKE A DOT

700 METRES
HEAD IS HARD TO SEE

This chart shows you what you can see of a person at
different distances.

Short Distances

MEASURE FROM TOE TO TOE

To work out short
distances, measure the
length of your stride.
Count your steps as you
walk along. Multiply the
number of steps by the
size of your stride to see
how far you have walked.

Things look further away when . . .

YOU LOOK AT THEM
ACROSS A VALLEY

YOU ARE KNEELING
OR LYING DOWN

YOU LOOK AT THEM
DOWN A STREET

THEY ARE IN THE SHADE

THEY ARE THE SAME
COLOUR AS BACKGROUND

THEY ARE IN MIST
OR DIM LIGHT

Things look closer when . . .

YOU LOOK AT THEM
ACROSS WATER

THE SUN IS
BEHIND YOU

THEY ARE UPHILL
OR DOWNHILL

THEY ARE BIGGER
THAN THINGS
AROUND THEM

THEY ARE A DIFFERENT
COLOUR FROM THE
BACKGROUND

YOU LOOK AT THEM
ACROSS A DEEP
CHASM

DO STREET
1 KILOMETRE

Long Distances

Use your watch to work out long distances. If it takes you 15 minutes to walk a kilometre, you know that after an hour you have walked about four kilometres. Practise as much as you can.

How Old Are They?

If you know the age, height and weight of different people, such as your family, it may help you guess how old, tall and heavy a suspect is. Remember—people change as they grow older. Their hair goes grey or they go bald. Very old people may be wrinkled and sometimes stoop when they stand.

Can you guess which of the descriptions below fits each of the people in the picture above?

Uncle Jeb is 42, weighs 69 kg and is 1.75 m tall.

Aunt Madge is 40, weighs 63.5 kg and is 1.6 m tall.

Brother Albert is almost 18. He weighs 79 kg and is 1.9 m tall.

Cousin Jessica is 30, weighs 51 kg and is 1.7 m.

Great Uncle Jake is 68, weighs 100 kg and is 1.80 m tall.

Great Aunt Hilda is 89, weighs 40 kg and is 1.5 m.

Brother John is 45, weighs 80 kg and is 1.9 m.

Grandfather Peel is 66, weighs 75 kg and is 1.82 m.

Answer

1. Great Uncle Jake 2. Uncle Jeb 3. Brother Albert 4. Grandfather Peel 5. Cousin Jessica 6. Great Aunt Hilda 7. Brother John 8. Aunt Madge